This book is ~~taken~~ given with love to...

To Audra and the kiddos at Good Shepherd Childcare Centre

From the creative mind of
Vince Cleghorne

Naughty Tim Sprocket

6'0"

5'6"

5'0"

4'6"

3'6"

2'6"

'6"

A Case of "Sticky" Fingers

This person, right here, **is Naughty Tim Sprocket...**

He stole things and stuffed them straight into his
pocket!

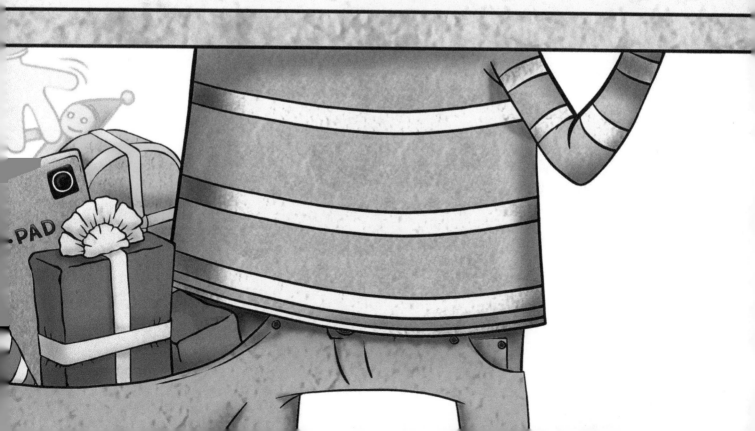

There really was nothing young Tim would not steal.

A hat from the **hat shop**...

...a bicycle wheel.

Or even the gifts
at a friend's birthday bash,
these went into his pocket
as quick as a flash!

GRRRR...

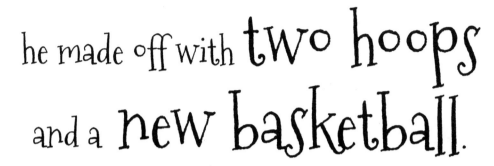

When Tim went to play at his local sports hall,
he made off with two hoops
and a new basketball.

Then one day on a visit with
Great Auntie Rose,
Tim was caught swiping money from under her nose.

Tim's parents were Shocked!

So off to the doctor's went Tim, Mom, and Dad,
with the hope for an answer...

to why
Tim's
gone
bad!

The doctor –

an expert on bad girls and boys,

who

Curse

Dr. Paisley Ketchup

Steal or Fight or who Like to make noise-

declared in a voice
that you might say was haughty,
"It's nobody's fault, your son is
just plain...

that his innocent surface was guilty beneath!

F!!!!"

Now his friends turned their backs
whenever they saw Tim,
when Tim called their names
they would simply ignore him.

While the bike store's alarm made Tim
run from the din!

OOOOGA!

WOO!

1-PAH!

RE!

And although Tim returned
all the things he once took,
for a long time, Tim Sprocket
was known as...

... TIM CROOK!

Now kids, just remember, don't take what's not yours!

Don't stuff goods in your pockets and run out the doors.

For if people can't trust you, it makes them feel sad,

your friends and your family, your mom and your dad...

So, when you see something that catches your eye,

and you're tempted to take it, just STOP and then try

kindly asking its owner if they'll let you borrow

that something 'til later, or maybe tomorrow!

The End

Claim Your FREE Gift!

Visit ➡ PDICBooks.com/Gift

Thank you for purchasing Naughty Tim Sprocket, and welcome to the Puppy Dogs & Ice Cream family.

We're certain you're going to love the little gift we've prepared for you at the website above.

CPSIA information can be obtained
at www.ICGtesting.com
Printed in the USA
BVHW021951140622
639651BV00025B/221